1989 Christmas
Merry Katie
Love, Eileen
Tim
Dan

THE
HIDING
BEAST

For Mary

Library of Congress Cataloging-in-Publication Data

Richardson, John, 1955–
    The hiding beast.

    Summary: A lonely boy's attempts to capture the
friendly beast that lives in the house he shares with
his aunt bring some happy changes in his life.
    [1. Monsters—Fiction. 2. Aunts—Fiction.
3. Friendship—Fiction] I. Title.
PZ7.R39487Hi 1988   [E]   88-9170
ISBN 0-395-49213-0

Copyright © 1988 by John Richardson

Published in the United States by Houghton Mifflin Company
Published in England by William Heinemann Ltd

Printed by Mandarin Offset in Hong Kong

10 9 8 7 6 5 4 3 2 1

THE HIDING BEAST

John Richardson

Houghton Mifflin Company
Boston   1988

Rodney was an orphan.
He lived with his Aunt Jocasta
in a grand and gloomy house.
He liked sliding down the banisters.
"Don't, dear," said Aunt Jocasta.
"You'll chip the paint."
He liked kicking his ball in the garden.
"Don't, dear," said Aunt Jocasta.
"You'll crush the flowers."
He liked playing armies in the billiard room.
"Don't, dear," said Aunt Jocasta.
"I can't abide the noise."

"What can I do, then?" said Rodney.
  Aunt Jocasta took him to the library.
"Read a nice, quiet book," she said.
  The first book Rodney found was
  about toads and lizards.
"Boring," said Rodney.
  The second book was about
  witches and wizards.
"Better," said Rodney.
  The next book was about ghosts
  and vampires.
"Great!" said Rodney.
  The last book was about beasts and
  monsters and wild, hairy things.
"Brilliant!" said Rodney.

That night, Rodney couldn't sleep.
He listened to the old clock, ticking
in the hall, and the snores of his aunt
in her bedroom far away.
Then he heard something else.
There was a shuffling, bumping, grunting noise,
a fumbling, stumbling, grumbling noise,
coming down the corridor toward his room.
Rodney hid under the blankets
and watched his bedroom door slowly open . . .

Aunt Jocasta was dreaming a boring
dream about tea parties and hairpins
and sensible shoes
when she woke up with a start.
"What was that noise?" she said.
"That bang? That crash?"
She climbed out of bed and wrapped
herself in a shawl.
"It's Rodney again, I suppose," she said.
"Drat the boy."

Rodney was shivering with excitement.
"Did you see him? Where's it gone?"
he shouted to his aunt.
"See who? Where's what gone?"
said Aunt Jocasta.
"The huge, wild, hairy thing, ten feet tall,
with great burning eyes and a
red and shiny nose," said Rodney.
"Rodney, don't talk nonsense,"
said Aunt Jocasta.
"You've been dreaming again."
Rodney fell asleep at last, but down in the
kitchen, something was moving about.

Next day, after breakfast, Rodney found a clue.
A trail of crumbs led out of the kitchen,
along the hall, past the dining room,
up the stairs, on and on to the top of the house.
And there, in the attic, sitting in a chair,
eating cookies off an old tin plate,
sat the wild and hairy thing, ten feet tall,
with great burning eyes and a red, shiny nose.

For a moment, the beast looked at Rodney,
and then he gave a terrified yell,
and leaped out of his chair, and onto the table,
and swung from the light, and over a chest,
and rushed out of the door, off and away,
down the stairs.

Rodney raced downstairs
and crashed into Aunt Jocasta.
"You must have seen him this time," he gasped.
"The wild and hairy thing, the hiding beast?"
His aunt looked stern.
"No beasts are allowed in my house," she said.
"But I saw him," said Rodney.
"Eating cookies in the attic."
"No cookies are allowed in my attic,"
said Aunt Jocasta.
"Now that's enough. Don't lie to me again, boy."

Rodney was sad.

He wanted to see the Hiding Beast again.

"I know. I'll make a trap for him," he said,
"like cavemen catch mammoths in books,
and hunters catch gorillas in jungles,
and spacemen catch aliens in films."
All morning, Rodney was very busy,
collecting everything
he needed for the beast trap.

After lunch, he set to work.

"Finished!" said Rodney at last.
"And now, Hiding Beast,
 I'm coming to get you!"
 He crept upstairs to the attic.
 No Hiding Beast up there.
 He peeped round the door of the library.
 Nothing but books in there.
 He searched through the
 bedrooms and bathrooms.
 Not a whisker or tail to be seen.
 He went back down to the kitchen
 and quietly opened the door.

What was that furry thing by the stove,
crouching down, clutching the cookie jar?
"Yaroo!" shouted Rodney at the top of his voice.
The thing was frightened and rushed away,
down the stairs, into the cellar,
and slap, bang, right into Rodney's trap.

"My beast! I've caught my beast!"
  yelled Rodney in delight.
  But then he stopped.
  The beast was turning around and
  looking at him.
  Rodney knew those eyes.
"Get me out of here," said the beast,
  and it sounded very cross.
  Rodney knew that voice.
"Aunt Jocasta!" he said.
"I thought . . . I thought you were a beast!"
  And then, the most amazing thing of all,
  Aunt Jocasta laughed.
"Oh, Rodney, Rodney," she gasped
  when she had wiped her eyes and
  got her breath back.
"You'll be the death of me.
  I'm not a beast, but I'm too old
  to bring up boys.
  It's time you went to school."
"School!" said Rodney. "Oh yes, please.
  When can I start? Tomorrow?"

That night, Rodney fell asleep at once,
and he dreamed a lovely dream,
about school friends and football
and mischief and games.
He never even heard the thump,
bump, on the stairs,
the shuffling and grunting,
the grumbling and fumbling
as a wild and hairy beast, the Hiding Beast,
stole down to the kitchen
in search of a midnight snack.

Nobody knows, nobody knows
Where the Hiding Beast comes from,
Or where he goes.
For the creature that loves
To steal and to feast
Is that clever, that cunning,
That shy Hiding Beast.